# CECIL
## The LOST SheeP

### CREATED BY ANDREW McDONOUGH

ZONDERVAN.com/
**AUTHORTRACKER**
*follow your favorite authors*

 ZONDER**kidz**

 LOST SheeP

What sort of animals does this man have?

Rabbits? No, he doesn't have rabbits.

Giraffes? Well, he might have giraffes,
but they don't get mentioned in this story.

Sheep? Yes, he has sheep.

One hundred sheep.

Including Cecil.

One day Cecil was daydreaming. "Boring, boring, boring. All I do is hang around with sheep, eat grass, wander down to the river for a little bit of a drink, and eat more grass. Maybe I could run away and, and…get a bike…or join a band!"

Cecil looked right.

Cecil looked left.

He jumped over his rock…

and hid.

From behind the rock
he snuck behind the tree,

and from behind the tree
he ran over the hills...

to the mountains!

Yes, the mountains!

He reached the mountains
and discovered they
were high and steep.

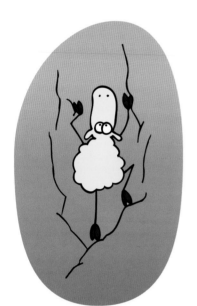

Cecil was not discouraged.
He began climbing
higher and higher,

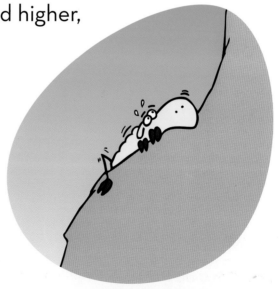

and it got steeper
and steeper...

and steeper.

He climbed and climbed until he couldn't climb up
and he couldn't climb down.

Cecil was stuck!

He sat on the edge of the ledge and started thinking.

"I could shout for help, but what will happen if
the shepherd finds me?
He might whack me with a big stick. CRACK!
Then grab me by the leg and drag me home.
BUMP, BUMP, BUMP.
And tie me to a tree without any dinner."

Back home the shepherd was counting his sheep.
"One, Michael. Two, Kevin. Three, Annette. Four,
Lucy…Ninety-six, Meredith. Ninety-seven, the other
Meredith. Ninety-eight, Abdul. Ninety-nine, Emily…

Cecil is missing!"

The shepherd ran to the rock
and found hoofprints leading
behind the tree.

He ran behind the tree and
found hoofprints leading
over the hills…

to the mountains!

Yes, the mountains!

The mountains were high and steep.

The shepherd climbed higher and higher, and it got steeper and steeper.

When he thought he couldn't climb any further and wasn't sure if he could climb back down, he heard a noise.

Cecil was saved!

What did the shepherd do?

Did he whack Cecil with his stick? *CRACK!*

No.

Did he grab Cecil by the leg and drag him
down the mountain? *BUMP, BUMP, BUMP.*

No.

He was so glad that he had found his lost sheep that he put Cecil on his shoulders and carried him home.

When they got home, did the shepherd tie Cecil to a tree without any dinner?

No. Instead he...

threw a huge party, and everyone
stayed up way past their bedtime.

Cecil, the lost sheep, had been found!

# Cecil's Page

*Cecil the Lost Sheep* (which is one of my favorite books, by the way) is based on Jesus' parable in Luke 15:1-7. You can use this story to teach children about God's love for them. You can also use this as a manual for teaching new shepherds just how well they should treat their beloved sheep...but that's for another day.

## Before the story

Begin by asking:
"Do you have a pet? How much do you love your pet?
"This much?" (Hold up your finger and thumb with a small gap between them.)
"This much?" (Hold up your hands with a bigger gap between them.)
"This much?" (Stretch your arms out wide.)
Then say, "Let me tell you one of Jesus' stories about how much God loves us."

## Read the story

## After the story

Say something such as, "How much do you think the shepherd loved Cecil? This much? This much? This much? OK, now if God is the shepherd and we are the sheep, how much do you think God loves you? This much? This much? This much?"

God's Blessings,
Cecil